R.L. 2.9

E   Ungerer, Tomi
Ung
           Crictor

DATE DUE		
NOV 02 1998		JAN 08 '06
JAN 28 1999		FEB 0
APR 13 1999		SEP 19 '07
DEC 12 2000		FEB
APR 09 2001		APR 14 08
FEB 25 2003		MAR 9 - '09
NOV 25 2003		NOV 4 '09
MAY 20 2004		NO 26 12
DEC 2 '05		JA 29

LL 720
RL 2.9
RC 6

IL K-3

GRL

10928

CONCORD OXBOW SCHOOL

9-73

tomi Ungerer

CRICTOR

HARPER & ROW, PUBLISHERS
NEW YORK, EVANSTON, AND LONDON

For Nancy, Ursula and Susan

CRICTOR
Copyright ©1958 by Jean Thomas Ungerer
Printed in the United States of America

All rights in this book are reserved.

Library of Congress catalog card number: 58-5288

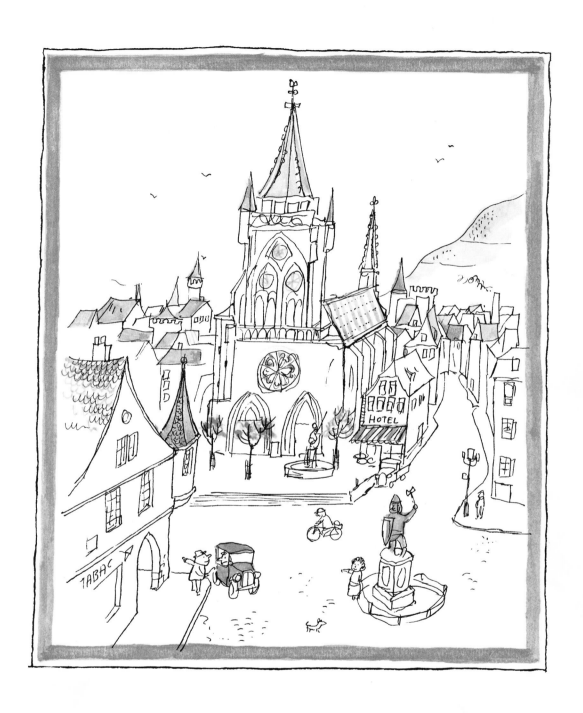

Once upon a time in a little French town

4   lived an old lady whose name was Madame Louise Bodot.

She had one son who was in Africa studying reptiles.

One morning the mailman brought her a peculiar O-shaped box.

Madame Bodot screamed when she opened it.

It was a snake her son had sent her for her birthday.

7

To make sure it was not a poisonous snake, she went to the zoo.

She identified it as a boa constrictor. So she called her animal

Crictor.

8

Madame Bodot mothered her new pet, feeding it bottles of milk.

She bought palm trees so Crictor would really feel at home.

As dogs do when they are happy, he wagged his tail.

Well fed, Crictor grew longer and longer and stronger and stronger. 11

The boa followed his mistress when she went shopping.

Everyone was astonished.

12

Madame Bodot knitted a long woolen sweater
for her pet to wear on cold days.

Crictor also had a warm, comfortable bed.

There he would dream happily, under his palm trees.

In the winter it was fun for Crictor to wriggle in the snow.

Madame Bodot taught at the public school.

One day she decided to take Crictor to her classes.

CONCORD OXBOW SCHOOL

Soon Crictor learned to shape the alphabet in his own way.

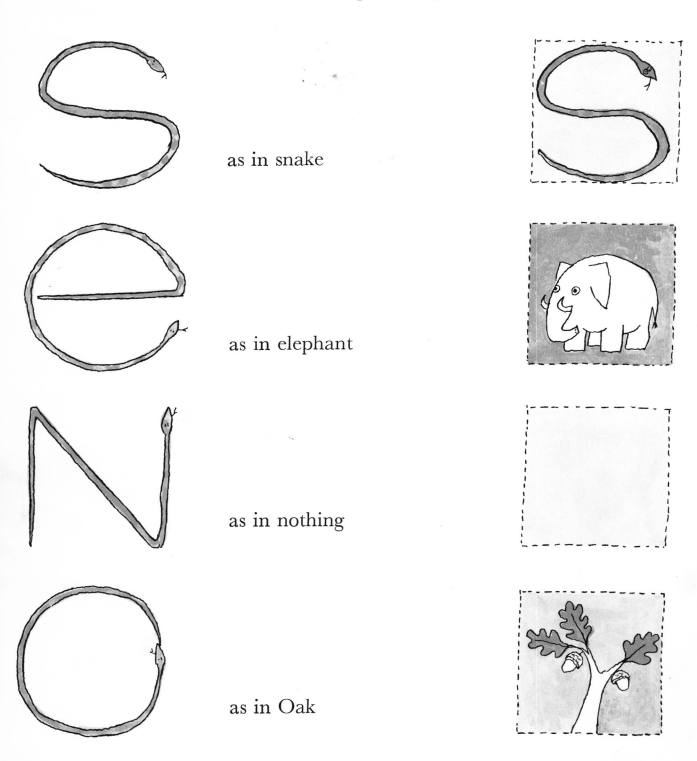

as in snake

as in elephant

as in nothing

as in Oak

18

as in lion

as in man

as in glass

as in whale

He could count too, forming figures.

 for your two hands

 for the three little pigs

 for the four legs of the dog

for your five fingers

 for the six legs of a bug

 for the seven dwarfs

 for the eight arms of the octopus

The boa liked to play with little boys

and little girls too.

He helped the boy scouts learn knots.

Crictor was a helpful snake.

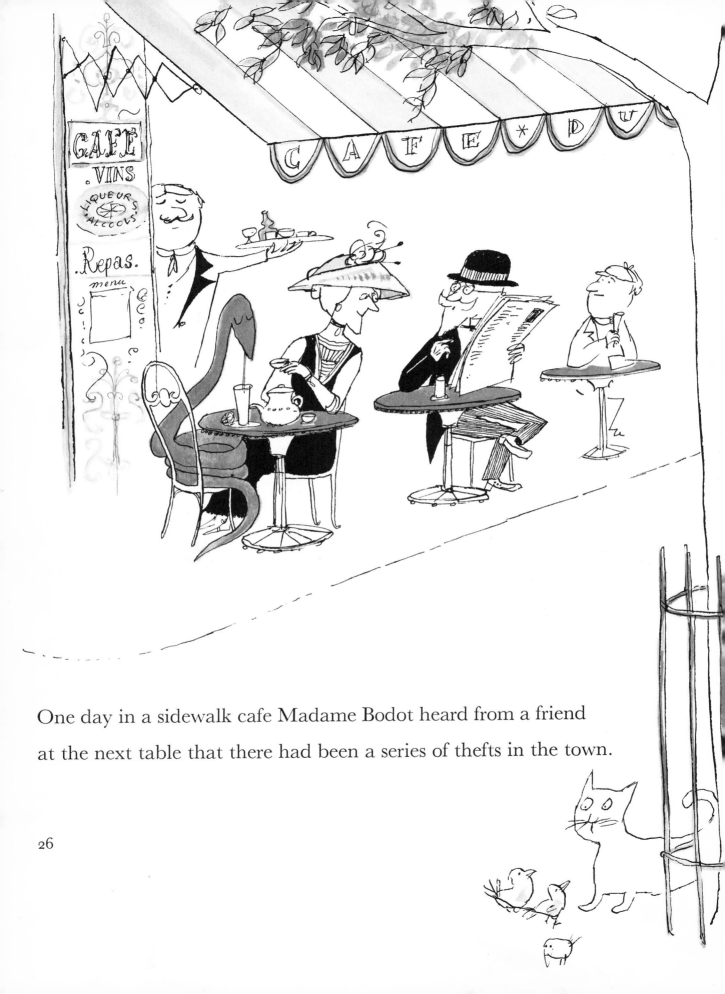

One day in a sidewalk cafe Madame Bodot heard from a friend
at the next table that there had been a series of thefts in the town.

That very night the burglar broke into her apartment.

Madame Bodot was already gagged and tied to a chair when the faithful boa awoke and furiously attacked the burglar. The villain's terrified shrieks awoke the neighbors.

Crictor remained coiled around him until the police arrived.   29

30   For his bravery a nice medal was awarded to the heroic snake.

Crictor even inspired the local sculptor to make a statue in his honor.

PARC CRICTOR

And the city dedicated a park to him.

Loved and respected by the entire village,

Crictor lived a long and happy life.

The End

CONCORD OXBOW SCHOOL